Lucy & Tom
at the Seaside

PUFFIN BOOKS

Published by the Penguin Group
Penguin Books Ltd, 27 Wrights Lane, London W8 5TZ, England
Penguin Books USA Inc., 375 Hudson Street, New York, New York 10014, USA
Penguin Books Australia Ltd, Ringwood, Victoria, Australia
Penguin Books Canada Ltd, 10 Alcorn Avenue, Toronto, Ontario, Canada M4V 3B2
Penguin Books (NZ) Ltd, 182–190 Wairau Road, Auckland 10, New Zealand

Penguin Books Ltd, Registered Offices: Harmondsworth, Middlesex, England

First published by Victor Gollancz Ltd 1976
Published in Picture Puffins 1993
Reissued in Puffin Books 1996
3 5 7 9 10 8 6 4 2

Copyright © Shirley Hughes, 1976
All rights reserved

Made and printed in Italy by Printers srl – Trento

Lucy & Tom
at the Seaside

SHIRLEY HUGHES

PUFFIN BOOKS

One hot day Lucy and Tom and their Mum and Dad
thought they would go to the seaside.
Lucy is helping to pack up the picnic. There are sandwiches
and hard-boiled eggs, apples, biscuits and a bottle of orange
squash. There is also a lovely chocolate cake.
Tom goes off to find the buckets and spades in the sandpit.

They go to the seaside in the train.
Tom keeps asking when they are going to get to the sea.
Lucy wears her armbands in the train so as to be all
ready to swim when they get there.
At last they've arrived! They walk down a rather
long road carrying all the picnic things and bathing bags
and buckets and spades.
There's a very special seasidey smell.

And there's the sea!

It's much, much bigger than either Lucy or Tom had ever remembered.

They run straight down to where the waves are coming up on to the wet sand and walk along the edge.

There are a lot of other children on the beach as well as mothers and fathers and babies and grannies and people paddling, and dogs who dash in and out of the water barking excitedly at seagulls.

Lucy and Tom want to swim right away, so they all put on
their bathing suits and go into the sea, hand in hand. Lucy
and Dad do some swimming. The sea is much rougher and
splashier than the swimming pool near home. It's harder to
swim in, but much more fun.

Tom likes being chased by the waves.

After the swim Mum helps everyone to rub dry and
they play a running-about game to get warm.
They settle down to their picnic.
Several wasps try to join in.

The tide is coming in.

Dad helps Lucy and Tom to make a beautiful sand castle. It
has turrets covered in shells and stones, a moat, and a tunnel
going right through the middle and coming out the
other side.

Slowly the moat fills up with water,
then the tunnel.

Soon only the top turret is left.

Then nothing at all.

A lot of interesting things are happening on the beach.
There are people flying kites and playing cricket and ball
games.
Two little girls are burying their father's legs in the sand so
that only his toes are sticking out.
Some people are trying to get in or out of their bathing suits
under towels, which is very difficult.

Lucy and Tom play in a rock-pool.
Lucy finds lots of different kinds of seaweed and
some shells which she puts
into her bucket.
Tom finds some stones and a crab's claw.

Lucy makes a face in the sand. It has stones for eyes,
a row of little shells for teeth,
and a lot of seaweedy hair.
Mum helps Tom make a speedboat pointing
right out to sea.

Further up the beach there are some donkeys. Lucy and Tom ask if they can have a ride.
Lucy's donkey is grey with white legs. His name – 'Pepsi' – is written on his harness.
Tom's donkey is brown and is called 'Cola'.

It's nearly time to go home.
Mum is packing up the picnic things.
There's just time for a last ice-cream.
Lucy writes her name in very big letters in the wet sand.
Then she writes Tom's name too.
It's been a *lovely* day.